D0549613

Ms MacDonald Has a Class

A Red Fox Book

Published by Random House Children's Books
20 Vauxhall Bridge Road, London SW1V 2SA

A division of Random House UK Ltd
London Melbourne Sydney Auckland
Johannesburg and agencues throughout the world

Copyright©Jan Ormerod 1996

3 5 7 9 10 8 6 4 2

First published in Great Britain by
The Bodley Head Childen'sBooks 1996

Red Fox edition 1998

The right of Jan Ormerod to be identified as the author of this
work has been asserted by her in accordance with the Copyright
Designs and Patents Act,1988.

Printed in China

RANDOM HOUSE UK Limited Reg.No. 954009

ISBN 0 09 951651 9

Ms MacDonald
Has a Class

Red Fox

Ms. MacDonald has a class, E-I-E-I-O,
She takes her class down to the farm, E-I-E-I-O,

With a pig pen here and a hay bale there,
Here a bucket, 'Where's your wellies?' everywhere a chick chick,

Ms MacDonald has a class, E-I-E-I-O.

Ms. MacDonald has a class, E-I-E-I-O,
And in that class they make some plans, E-I-E-I-O,

With a "What's this?" here and a "Do what?" there,
Here a chatter, there a natter, everywhere a pitter patter,
Ms. MacDonald has a class, E-I-E-I-O.

Ms. MacDonald has a class, E-I-E-I-O,
And in that class they flip flap flop, E-I-E-I-O,

With a skip trip here and a hop step there,
Here a jump, there a bump, everywhere a boing boing,

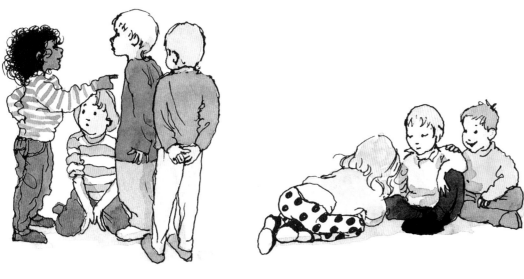

A "What's this?" here and a "Do what?" there,
Here a chatter, there a natter, everywhere a pitter patter,
Ms. MacDonald has a class, E-I-E-I-O.

Ms. MacDonald has a class, E-I-E-I-O,
And in that class they sing along, E-I-E-I-O,

With a tra-la here and a tra-la there,
Here a tra, there a la, everywhere a tra-la,

A skip trip here and hop step there,
Here a jump, there a bump, everywhere a boing boing,

A "What's this?" here and a "Do what?" there,
Here a chatter, there a natter, everywhere a pitter patter,
Ms. MacDonald has a class, E-I-E-I-O.

Ms. MacDonald has a class, E-I-E-I-O,
And in that class they make some sounds, E-I-E-I-O,

With a boom boom here and a ting-a-ling there,
Here a boom, there a ting, everywhere a boom-a-ling,

A tra-la here and a tra-la there,
Here a tra, there a la, everywhere a tra-la,

A skip trip here and a hop step there,
Here a jump, there a bump, everywhere a boing boing,

A "What's this?" here and a "Do what?" there,
Here a chatter, there a natter, everywhere a pitter patter,

Ms. MacDonald has a class, E-I-E-I-O.

Ms. MacDonald has a class, E-I-E-I-O,
And in that class they snip and stitch, E-I-E-I-O,

With a snip snip here and a stitch stitch there,
Here a snip, there a stitch, everywhere a snip stitch,

A boom boom here and a ting-a-ling there,
Here a boom, there a ting, everywhere a boom-a-ling,

With a tra-la here and a tra-la there,
Here a tra, there a la, everywhere a tra-la,

A skip trip here and a hop step there,
Here a jump, there a bump, everywhere a boing boing,

A "What's this?" here and a "Do what?" there,
Here a chatter, there a natter, everywhere a pitter patter,
Ms. MacDonald has a class, E-I-E-I-O.

Ms. MacDonald has a class, E-I-E-I-O,
And in that class they paint and glue, E-I-E-I-O,

With a slap slop here and a splish splash there,
Here a slop, there a splash, everywhere a drip drop,

A snip snip here and a stitch stitch there,
Here a snip, there a stitch, everywhere a snip stitch,

A boom boom here and a ting-a-ling there,
Here a boom, there a ting, everywhere a boom-a-ling,

A tra-la here and a tra-la there,
Here a tra, there a la, everywhere a tra-la,

A skip trip here and a hop step there,
Here a jump, there a bump, everywhere a boing boing,

A "What's this?" here and a "Do what?" there,
Here a chatter, there a natter, everywhere a pitter patter,
Ms. MacDonald has a class, E-I-E-I-O.

Ms. MacDonald has a class, E-I-E-I-O,
And in that class they tidy up, E-I-E-I-O,

With the paper here and the scissors there,
Here a lid, there a wipe, everybody wash hands,

A "Yum yum" here and a "Yum yum" there,
Here a "Yum," there a "Yum," everywhere a "Yum yum,"

A "SHHH" here and a "SHHH" there,
Here a "SHHH," there a "SHHH," everywhere a ZZZ-ZZZ,
Ms. MacDonald has a class, E-I-E-I-O.

Ms. MacDonald has a class, E-I-E-I-O,
And in that class they're almost there, E-I-E-I-O,

With a "One chair here?" and a "Two chairs there?"
Here a plink, there a plonk, everywhere a "Watch out!"

A fluffy tail here and a spotty face there,
Here a "Ready," there a "Steady," everywhere a "Let's Go!"

A moo moo here and a moo moo there,
Here a brmm, there a brmm, everywhere a cheep cheep,

A scarecrow here and a crow crow there,
Here a cluck, there a squawk, everywhere a cockle-doodle,

A woof woof here and a baa baa there,
Here a baa, there a baa, everywhere a baa baa,

An oink oink here and an oink oink there,
Here a hop, there a waddle, everywhere a quack quack,

A gobble gobble here and a gobble gobble there,

Here a nip, there a nip, everywhere a run run...

Ms. MacDonald has a class, E-I-E-I-O· · · · ·

Ms. MacDonald has a class, E-I-E-I-O,
And in that class they take a bow, E-I-E-I-O,
With a clap clap here and a clap clap there,
Here a clap, there a clap, everywhere a "Hooray!"

Ms. MacDonald has a class, E-I-E-I-O.